CONTENTS

Chapter 1

A Mother for Her Children

James put his arm round his little sister Belle. She was crying, and James didn't want her to cry, but what could he say to comfort her? He couldn't tell her their mammy was going to get better – she wasn't. He couldn't tell her things were going to be fine – they weren't. Things would never be fine again.

"Why can't we go up and see Mammy, James?" William asked. He was only a year older than Belle. He didn't understand what was happening either.

"Mrs Carter told us to stay down here in her house," James told him.

"But I don't like her house," William said.

James didn't blame him. He didn't like Mrs Carter's house either. It was two floors below theirs and it was a cold, clean place, with no fire in the grate.

Their house was cosy. Mammy always had a fire lit.

"You must have money to burn," Mrs Carter would say to Mammy in her nippy voice.

Mrs Carter was always trying to boss Mammy about. She was never away from their door with her complaints.

"That Belle's making too much noise."

"They should be in bed at this time of night."

Today, James knew he should be grateful to Mrs Carter. She'd helped to look after Mammy when Mammy took sick and had to go to her bed. But Mrs Carter never let them forget it.

"Your layabout father should be here," she would say.

"He's not a layabout," James would tell her. "He's a soldier."

But Mrs Carter was right. His father should be here. But Mammy refused to send for him.

"I'll soon be better," she kept saying.

But James knew from the look of her pale skin and dull eyes that she wasn't getting better.

It hadn't always been like this. James could remember better times, happier times. When his father was here. Those days seemed like a dream now, but it wasn't so long ago. Dad would come home from his work on the railway and he'd run out to the street and play football with them. Sometimes he'd lift little Belle on his back and chase James and William, pretending to be a wild monster. James could still hear Belle giggling with joy.

Their mammy would stand at the front door and watch. She'd have just come from the wash house and she'd have a scarf tied round her hair and a big pile of washing in a basket. James could almost see her now, her cheeks red from the steam in the wash house, her face lit up with a big smile.

The image faded.

Everything changed when Dad lost his job, and he couldn't get another one. Then there was no more football, no more fun, no more monster games with Belle on Dad's back. The arguments started, and their dad would storm out of the house in a rage and James wouldn't hear him come back before he fell asleep.

James had heard the final argument, though.

Their angry voices had woken him.

His mammy didn't sound like herself at all. Her voice was always soft and warm, but that night it was harsh and cold as ice. "I'm fed up with this," she said. "All I do is scrimp and save to feed Belle and James and William."

His dad shouted back. "Well, you won't have to put up with me much longer!" Then James heard him take a deep breath. "I've joined up," he said. "I'm a soldier now."

James couldn't see his mammy's face, but he knew by the long time it took for her to answer that she was shocked. "So, you're just going to leave me here with the wee ones, are you?" he heard her ask.

"Och, you can manage," his dad said. "You don't need me. And at least I can send some money home."

And then he had gone. James knew the army wanted men to fight in the war. But he hadn't thought that his dad would be gone so fast. Just like that. James hadn't seen him since. He'd written, and he'd sent some money.

Mammy read the letter out to them almost every night.

Tell my James and William and Belle that I am proud of them all, and I miss them. Every night I look up at the stars and it comforts me to know you're all looking at those same stars. James, you're the man of the house now. You must look after your brother and sister, and help your mammy. I miss her too. And one day, I promise, we will all be together again.

James had seen how his mammy kept that letter on the shelf above the fire, behind the clock. He had seen how she took it out after they were in bed, when she thought they were all asleep, and read it over and over.

"Where's my daddy now?" he asked her one night, when Belle and William were asleep. He had crept out of bed to sit with her in front of the fire. She had a fit of coughing before she could answer him. The cough was getting worse and worse.

"Well, James," she said when she could speak again. "He's signed on at Maryhill Barracks. After he's done his training, he'll be away to the Front."

"The front of what?" James asked, and that had made Mammy smile. "When's he coming back?"

"When the war's over," she had told him.

But the war wasn't over yet and James had found out what the Front was. It was where the worst of the fighting happened. James didn't like the idea of his dad being there one bit. He'd heard boys in his school say some soldiers never came back from the Front, or if they did, they came back shells of men. It scared him to think that might happen to his daddy.

Chapter 2

Tables of Home

Mammy died.

Soldiers died at the Front, but Mammy died at home. Their home, on the top floor of the tenement.

James didn't tell William and Belle, not the night it happened. And when at last they had to know, on the day of the funeral, he just said, "She's with the angels."

That made Belle happy. She loved angels.

Mrs Carter had let them stay on at her house.

"You're such a good woman," the other women all said. "The way you took in those poor wee souls when their mother was sick."

Mrs Carter smiled a thin-lipped smile that said she agreed with them.

'Should I think she's a good woman too?' James wondered. No, it seemed to him she was nothing more than an old witch.

"Isn't anybody going to get my dad?" James asked Mrs Carter on the day of the funeral.

"Him?" Mrs Carter said. "Not a soul knows where he is."

"He's away to be a soldier," James told her. He stood up straight, proud of his dad.

Mrs Carter sneered at that. Her face crunched up like a withered apple, and she really did look like a witch. "Soldier?" she mocked. "Him? He'll have run away already."

That made James mad. "No, he won't," he shouted. "My daddy's a hero."

"Some hero," Mrs Carter said. "Left his wife and three wee ones to look after themselves."

James almost told her about the letter then, but he stopped himself at the last moment. He had a picture in his mind of what would happen if he did. Mrs Carter would go upstairs, take the letter, read it and then throw it on the fire. It would be gone for ever. It was their only link to their dad. So he said nothing.

"When can we go back home?" William asked.

It was the day after the funeral. They were still at Mrs Carter's house, with its polished black grate, cold as a grave. 'Just like Mrs Carter,' James thought. He hadn't asked her when they could go home. He was afraid of the answer.

"The rent on your house is paid up till tomorrow," Mrs Carter told them. "Then there's another family ready to move in."

"But what about all our stuff?" James asked.

"Stuff? Rubbish more like," she said. "You can go up and get what you need."

Belle began to cry. "Are we going to have to stay with you for ever, Mrs Carter?"

William began to cry then too, terrified by the thought of a life in this harsh, cold house.

"Stay with me?" Mrs Carter looked as terrified as William. Her false teeth began to chatter at the idea. "No, no, no," she said. "You three will have to go into a home."

"No!" James cried. He shook his head. "You only go into a home if you're an orphan. We've got a father!"

Mrs Carter stared down into his face. He could see that the skin on her nose was flecked with little holes and her top lip was fuzzy with the trace of a moustache. James didn't like to be this close to her.

"Where is your father then?" she hissed.

James didn't have an answer to that. "He's away to be a soldier," he mumbled. It was all he could say.

Later that day, they went up the stairs to their old home. James tried not to cry at the memories of the happy times they'd had here. But it was so hard. He could almost see

his mammy standing at the sink, washing the dishes and singing. She was always singing.

He could still hear her, her soft voice like a ghost in the air.

We were sailing along, on Moonlight Bay.

That was her favourite.

And there was the bed where their father would tuck them in and tell them stories. James wanted to cry, but he couldn't. If he started, so would William. And then Belle. He had to be strong for them.

They gathered up their few belongings, the cardigans their mammy had knitted for them, and Belle's ribbons, and they stuffed them into a big bag that Mammy had kept under the sink. William clutched at the toy train his daddy had made for him, and he wouldn't let it go.

"Have you got everything?" James asked. He took one last look round the single room he had called home all his life.

"Yes," William said. "But I'm scared."

"Can't we live here together?" Belle said. "You're a big boy, James, you could look after us. I don't want to go to a home. Where will I keep my ribbons?"

"I know," James whispered, with a squeeze of her hand. He had to be brave for Belle and William, but what could he do to stop Mrs Carter taking them to that gloomy place where the orphans lived? Every time James walked past it he always crossed the street, sure someone was waiting inside ready to reach out and drag him in. He could see the orphans standing at the windows, and they always looked sad.

James let go of Belle's hand and walked over to the fireplace. The ashes were cold in the grate now, but he could remember when the fire would roar and his dad would stick bread on a long fork and hold it against the flames to toast it for their supper. And that was when he saw the letter behind the clock on the mantle shelf. He'd almost forgotten it. He snatched it up, and held it so hard he almost crushed it. An idea had begun to form in his mind. He smiled at his brother and sister.

"We're not going into a home," he told them. "We're going to find our daddy."

CHAPTER 3

In the Morning

———

"A letter, you say?" Mrs Carter eyed James, as if she knew he was telling a lie. "So when did this letter arrive?"

"It came this morning," James told her. "It was on the floor when we went up the stairs."

"Funny, I never heard the postman," Mrs Carter said. "Let me see it."

She tried to snatch the letter from him, but James stepped away from her and held it tighter in his fist.

"It's private," he said. "It's from our father." Then he did hold it up for her, just so she could see the address on it was his mammy's. He took a deep breath. He'd never told such a lie before. "It says we've to come and stay with him."

"Stay with him?" There was a nasty smile on Mrs Carter's face. "And where would that be?"

James wouldn't let her get the better of him. He had thought it all out. "The army have got him a house," he said. "We've to stay there."

"I thought he was away fighting?"

"He is. But they're sending him back to look after us."

Mrs Carter laughed then. She had a horrible laugh, as if there was a cat being strangled in her throat. "Well, I'm sure we can't win this war without your father there fighting. The Front will collapse without him."

And she strangled the cat in her throat a bit more as she laughed at her own nasty joke.

James looked at her and remembered a phrase he had heard his teacher say. "He's getting passionate leave," he told her.

"Compassionate leave!" Mrs Carter corrected him, but she must have known what he meant because she nodded. "Oh, I see," she said. Her nostrils flared as if she was smelling something rotten, and the something rotten was James.

But James could tell she wanted to believe him. If they went to their father, she would be rid of them. Everyone would still say what a good woman she was. She would have done her duty and she would be happy.

"Oh well, you're better off with your father, I suppose," she said, at last.

"We're really going to live with my daddy?" Belle whispered when Mrs Carter had gone.

William answered her. "Did you not hear James, Belle? Our daddy sent us a letter."

James hated to lie to them, but he couldn't tell them the truth. It would only scare them. And if Mrs Carter wanted rid of the three of them, then they would go. James was determined not to let his brother and sister go into any home.

"Aye, Belle, we're going to our daddy," he told her. His voice was as determined and grown-up as he could make it.

Belle was so happy that she leaped up into his arms and hugged him.

CHAPTER 4

Against Odds Uncounted

"You're sure that daddy of yours will be there to meet you?" Mrs Carter asked.

She had given them some bread and margarine for the journey. She'd even helped to pack the bag they were taking with them, although she had slapped Belle when she took her ribbons out again. Five minutes later, James heard another neighbour telling her again what a wonderful woman she was.

"You've opened the door to Heaven for yourself with your kindness to those poor souls," the neighbour told her.

Mrs Carter swelled up like a big fat hen and smiled.

"It's the least I could do," she said, and James could almost see her preening her feathers.

James told himself he should be grateful. Mrs Carter had believed their story. She'd even told the neighbours about the letter from their daddy, as if she had read it herself. He'd heard her say "compassionate leave" more than once. No one asked anything else after that.

So now they were ready to go. Belle jumped up and down, her face bright with happiness. "We're going to my daddy," she kept saying. Then she clutched at James's hand and would not let go.

'Am I doing the right thing?' James wondered. He was telling them a lie. But it was a lie that was going to save them in the end.

His dad trusted him to look after his brother and sister. And James would not let his dad down.

James had told Mrs Carter their dad would be waiting for them at Maryhill Barracks.

"Do you know how to get there?" Mrs Carter asked again. "I suppose I could go with you."

James almost choked. "No! I mean, no, Mrs Carter. That's kind of you, but I'm a big boy now. I can look after my brother and sister." And then he added, "Thank you. You've done enough for us." He knew that would please her.

Mrs Carter didn't need him to say it twice. James knew that she hadn't wanted to go anyway, but she had asked in the hope that the door to Heaven would swing open even wider.

James remembered his mammy, and he knew what she would have wanted him to do.

What she had taught them to do. Always say thank you, always be respectful to older people.

"Thank you for everything, Mrs Carter," James said again.

"I always like to do the right thing," she clucked.

She stood at the window and watched the three of them as they walked up the street, hand in hand. James could feel her eyes on them the whole way. Only William turned round. "Will I wave to her, James?" he asked.

James shrugged. "Mammy would want you to," he said.

And William waved, then he looked up at James.

"She didn't wave back," he said.

Chapter 5

Hopes Profound

James had a plan. He knew where the station was – he'd gone there once with his dad to collect his pay. It was a fair way from where they lived, but he could ask one of the men who worked at the station how they could get to Maryhill Barracks. If it was someone who remembered their dad, they might even get a lift there.

Dad had signed on at Maryhill Barracks – that's what James's mammy had told him. He would speak to the officers there and tell them how their mammy had died and they would find his dad for them. James was sure of it.

The three of them walked for a long time across fields and over stiles and down long streets. There were posters everywhere about the war.

FOLLOW ME.

YOUR COUNTRY NEEDS YOU.

JOIN NOW.

At last, Belle stopped and flopped onto the ground. "I'm tired," she said.

James lifted her and tried to carry her for a while. But she was heavy and he was tired too. It was getting dark – it must be late. Nights in May were always long and light. All at once James saw a picture of his dad in the street, with his sleeves rolled up and his braces hanging down, playing football with them, till Mammy came and shouted them in for bed.

"Are you crying, James?" William sounded scared and he would be scared if he thought his big brother was crying. James blinked away the tears.

"Something in my eye, that's all." James looked around. They were at the station at last, but it was deserted. Not a soul about. Mammy had always warned them about going near the trains. But there was one on a siding, standing idle and empty. It was an old train with wooden carriages. Not nearly as grand as some of the others James had seen.

William held up his toy train. "It's not half as good as mine," he said.

James smiled. "No, it isn't, William. But if we can get in there, we'll have somewhere to sleep. Then in the morning we'll find somebody to take us to the Barracks."

The train had a long line of carriages, with walls between each separate set of seats in each carriage. They were all locked up, but James saw a crack in the window of one of them. He looked around to make sure there was still no one about, and then, with his elbow, he banged hard on the glass and it shattered.

They stood for a moment in case someone came running, someone who had heard the window break. But no one came. With a sigh of relief, James lifted William up and in the window.

"Watch you don't cut yourself," he warned. But William was inside in a moment, then he leaned out of the window to help Belle.

There were two long seats facing each other, just like two beds. 'We can easily sleep here,' James thought.

Once they were all settled, Belle and William giggled, and James knew why. This was like one of the adventures their daddy used to tell them. He was always telling them stories, about being chased by lions in the jungle or having a shoot-out with outlaws like the cowboys in the Wild West. And here they were now, having a real adventure.

"Wait till we tell Daddy about this," James whispered to them.

James still had some of the bread and margarine that Mrs Carter had given them, and he shared it out. He made sure William and Belle had more than him. His father would want him to do that. And then he could see Belle's eyes closing with tiredness. He lifted her and laid her along one of the seats.

"You sleep there, Belle," he said.

She tugged at his arm. "Tell us a story, James," she said. "Please."

That made William open his eyes wide. "Yes, tell us a story," he begged.

So James settled on the floor with William close beside him and began to tell them a story, just the way their daddy and their mammy used to. A story about an adventure, with two knights and a beautiful princess called Belle, who had to face all sorts of dangers as they tried to find their way through a dark forest.

They were both asleep long before the story was over. William's head rested on James's knees and Belle snored on the seat, but James finished the story anyway. The knights and princess were lost, but they followed the stars and the stars led them to safety.

James wanted to make sure their story had a happy ending.

Chapter 6

Hidden from Sight

The tooting of the whistle and the rocking of the train woke James. They were moving! He slipped William from his knee and stood up. It was dark outside, but James could still see fields and hills as the train rolled past. They would never be able to jump off. The train was moving too fast and James couldn't take a risk like that with little Belle. They would just have to see where the train took them.

"Where are we going?" was the first thing Belle said when she woke up.

"It's an adventure, Belle," James told her. "We just have to wait and see."

He gave them the last of the bread, but he could tell from the hungry look on their faces that it wasn't enough.

"We'll get food as soon as we stop," James said. "I promise."

They had never been on a train before. James made a game where they ran from one side to the other so they could look out all the windows. It made them forget how hungry they were.

After a while, the train began to slow down. James realised that they were coming into a station.

"As soon as the train stops and the driver gets out, that's when we get out too," James told Belle and William.

Belle sat on the seat and kicked her legs with excitement.

But getting out would be harder than they thought. They couldn't jump onto the platform in case someone saw them, and the broken window they had come in was now on the wrong side, where it was a long drop to the track. Much too high for Belle.

"What's that noise?" Belle said. "Listen! Can you hear it?"

James listened. "It's bagpipes," he said. "I'm sure it is."

The skirl of the music lifted James's heart. It was bagpipes, and the sound was coming closer and closer.

James looked out of the window and saw them marching into view. Soldiers. All in their khaki uniforms, rifles slung over their shoulders. Hundreds of them, led by pipers. There were drummers too, and lots of other people. Some were waving banners and flags as they marched along beside the soldiers, singing and cheering.

"It's soldiers," William shouted.

"Soldiers! Soldiers!" Belle cried. She jumped up, but she was too small to see out of the window and along the platform. "Is my daddy with them?"

'If only he could be,' James thought. 'If only I could look into that swell of soldiers and see our daddy marching with them. Then I would grab Belle and William and run to him, and everything would be all right.'

Maybe their daddy was with them. There were so many of them that it was hard to tell.

"What are we going to do, James?" William asked.

"The soldiers are coming on the train," James said. "When they do, we'll ask them to help us."

He was sure that was the right thing to do. The soldiers would help them. The soldiers might even know their dad.

They peered through the window and watched the soldiers march to a halt, then stand to attention. The bagpipes stopped playing and the air seemed lonely without their music.

An important-looking man with a gold chain round his neck came forward. He made a speech, and everyone cheered when he finished. Then the bagpipes started up again, the soldiers swung their kit bags on their backs and they all began to climb onto the train.

James looked around. "I think we'd better hide till they're all on board," he said. "They might throw us off and then we'd be in trouble if that man with the gold chain catches us."

Belle's chin began to tremble. She was ready to cry. James patted her back. "There's nothing to cry about, Belle," he said. "We'll hide under the seats and when the train starts moving again, we'll ask if the soldiers know our daddy. The soldiers will help us. Who knows, our daddy might even be on this train."

Chapter 7

Staunch to the End

They all hid under the seat. James could feel Belle's little body shaking. He pulled her tight against him and stroked her face to comfort her. William squeezed under the long seat across from them. James could see his wee face. William was holding in the tears, trying to be brave.

"Please let my dad not be at the Front," James prayed. "Please let him be here. Let my dad be on this train."

They could hear the soldiers singing, shouting and laughing as they jumped into each carriage and took their seats. The train was filling up fast. Soon, a group of soldiers threw themselves down on the seats where James and the little ones were hiding.

Kit bags landed with a thump on the floor or high up in the luggage racks, and the soldiers leaned out of the window to wave to the people on the platform who had come to see them off. And all the time the bagpipes played.

'If only I could be a soldier like my dad,' James thought. 'One day, I will be.'

Belle jumped when a big pair of boots clumped down on the floor beside them. James put a finger to her lips to keep her quiet. He didn't want anyone to find them now – not till the train moved off. He could imagine that man with the gold chain would grab them, march them to the nearest children's home or, even worse, the poor house. A man like that wouldn't listen to them when they said that they were going to find their father, or that

they weren't orphans. Even if James waved the letter in his face it wouldn't matter. That man looked clever, and he would see that the letter had nothing to do with them going to meet their father.

No, they had to wait here, silent, and after the train moved off they would come out of their hiding place and ask the soldiers to help them and ...

James's spirits lifted again with the skirl of the bagpipes and the beat of the drums. The sound gave him hope they would find their dad. Of course they would. Or they would find someone who knew him. James had to believe that. And if he believed it enough, it would be true.

As the train pulled out of the station the bagpipes were playing a tune James knew.

Will ye no' come back again?

James could hear the crowds on the platform singing, and the soldiers joining in. And then James felt like crying again, because he knew that some of those brave young soldiers never would come back again.

The singing and the cheering on the platform faded into the distance. After a while, the soldiers settled down.

James still didn't move. He wanted to wait till they'd gone far enough that no one would stop the train and send them back. He kept thinking about that man with the chain. In James's mind, the man's face became the face of Mrs Carter as she loomed over James with her black-flecked nose and her withered cheeks and her rattling false teeth. There would be no pity in the man with the chain, just as there was no pity in Mrs Carter. He would not listen to the pleas of James or William. He would not be moved by wee Belle's tears.

Then, all of a sudden, Belle let out a yell when the soldier with the big boots tried to stuff his kit bag under his seat. The soldier dropped to his knees and peered under.

"What have we here?" he said.

Chapter 8

Their Laughing Comrades

Belle began to cry. William froze. James crawled out and stood up. He made himself as tall as he could. "We're looking for our father," he said. "Please don't throw us off the train."

The tears rolled down Belle's face. The soldier reached out for her and helped her up from under the seat. "There, there, lass," he said. "Nobody's going to throw you off the train. Or you, wee man." He reached out for William, who was still hiding under the opposite seat. William was smiling when he emerged, still clutching his toy train. The other soldiers began to laugh.

"We have our mascots!" someone shouted.

"My name's Toby," the big soldier told them. "And tell me, what's your dad's name?"

James told him. "Same name as me," he finished, proud. He looked around. "Does anybody know him?"

"And what makes you think your dad's on this train?" Toby asked.

James wanted to give him a good answer. "He's going to the Front, or he's already there," he said. "He's a soldier."

"Well, we're all headed to the Front too, but this train isn't stopping till we get to Liverpool," Toby said.

"Where's Liverpool?" William asked.

Belle didn't say a word. She was looking at the big sandwich one of the soldiers was munching on. He stopped eating and looked at her. "You hungry, wee one?"

He didn't wait for an answer. He handed over the sandwich. "Here, you all look hungry."

Toby called to the other soldiers. "Hey, any spare food for these wee ones?"

James smiled. Hadn't he said the soldiers would help them? Soon they were eating hungrily and Toby gave them all some water to drink from his flask.

"Right," Toby said. "Now tell us about this dad of yours."

So James told him about their dad going off to be a soldier, then he told him about their mammy, and Belle cuddled against him at that bit, and he told him how they were going to find their dad so they wouldn't have to go into a home.

"I think he's a Captain," James said at the end of his story.

"A Captain, you say. Bet he is," Toby said and he looked at the other soldiers and smiled. "Well, James, we can't do much at the moment. We're stuck in here till we get to Liverpool. But when we do, we're going to find your dad for you. And if he's not on this train, the army will find out where he is for you."

Toby ruffled James's hair. Most times he hated it when a big person did that, but now he didn't mind. William was laughing too, munching on bread, and Belle's face was full of smiles. "We're going to find our daddy, aren't we, James?" they both said.

"Now," Toby said. "I think you three should lie down and have a wee nap. I think you deserve it."

The soldiers all squeezed up to give them room. James sat with Belle across his lap, and William cuddled up beside him.

'There's something magical about this train,' James thought, as he looked around. The light from the gas lamps gave the carriage a yellow glow, and the soldiers seemed to him to be bathed in gold. The soldiers were special. He had known they would help them. They had shared their food with them. They were going to help them find their daddy.

Toby leaned across and patted his arm. "You're a good big brother, James," he said.

"He's the best brother in the world," Belle agreed.

James felt contented as he drifted off to sleep. He had done the best he could. They would find their dad soon, or their dad would find them.

CHAPTER 9

When We Are Dust

In another carriage, a young soldier was also trying to sleep. But he couldn't. He was too scared. He'd heard stories about what happened in the trenches. Men went over the top, ran towards the enemy alongside their comrades and watched them fall as the bullets hit them. They weren't able to stop to help, they had to keep running. Could he do that? He looked around at the other soldiers beside him. Some of them were playing cards, or chatting. How could they look so calm? He wished he could be as brave and fearless as they seemed to be on their way to this terrible war.

At last he drifted off, thinking of the sweetheart he had left behind. Thinking of his young brother too, so eager to become a soldier like him. But his brother was 15 – and by the time he was 17, this war would be over. It had to be.

It was the impact that woke him. He felt as if he had been flung against a brick wall. He was thrown from his seat. They all were. He was hurled across the carriage and his head cracked against the opposite wall. Rifles and kit bags tumbled from the racks.

"We've crashed!" one of the soldiers yelled.

The young soldier tumbled to the floor, his body in a broken heap. He put his hand to his head and when he took it away it was covered in wet, sticky blood.

The soldiers all around him were making frantic efforts to get out. They shook the doors, banged on them and tugged at the handles. It was no use. The doors were locked.

The young soldier could do nothing. Around him, the air was filled with shouts of fury and of fear.

"Break a window!" a voice shouted.

There was no time. No time for anything.

The young soldier heard the whistle and he knew there was another train screeching towards them, trying desperately to stop. The others heard it too.

Panic set in. Soldiers pushed at doors, tried to break windows, tried to escape – but it was too late.

The whole carriage was thrown into the air. The young soldier was flying. He was flying into an explosion of flames as the fire began to rage.

His last thought was that he would never have to face the war now. He would never be a soldier.

Chapter 10

There Is Music

James was standing on the embankment, Belle's hand clutched in his. He looked around for William and breathed a sigh of relief when he saw his little brother running towards them.

"What happened, James?" William asked.

James shook his head. "There's been a crash. A terrible crash."

He put his hand across Belle's eyes. He didn't want her to see the fire, or the bodies lying on the grass. He didn't want to look himself. But when he did look, he seemed to be seeing them through some kind of haze.

James was glad. He couldn't hear anything properly either. The sounds of men shouting, the screams, the crackle of fire seemed distant. As if they were coming from far away.

"Can you see Toby?" William asked. He was looking around, but curling smoke seemed to be gathering around them, and it was hard to make anyone out.

"Toby will be helping the others," James told him. He was sure that was true. "Come on. I think we should get as far away as possible."

James took William's hand and led him and Belle up the embankment. He told them not to look at the bodies that were lying there. He tried not to look either.

They saw a young soldier staggering up the embankment. Blood was pouring from his head.

"Look, there's people coming to help," James said. If he peered through the smoke he could see farm workers and villagers racing towards the scene. One of them caught the young soldier just as he was about to fall.

The people ignored the children, running past them without a look. James thought that was strange, but – of course – there were so many injured soldiers and they were the ones who needed help.

"I don't like it here," Belle said. "Why do I feel so funny, James?" And she cuddled into him.

"I know," James said. "I feel strange too. I don't think we should stay here. We'll head for the village." James could see it in the distance, the spire of the church dark against the bright blue sky. "We'll be safe there."

James wanted to get his sister and his brother as far away from this place as he could. There was nothing they could do to help. And he hated the cries and the screaming, and the smell. Yet everything seemed to be fading, smothered by the mist of smoke.

"Listen," William said. "I can hear birds singing."

"Me too," Belle said.

James could hear the birds too, clear as a bell. It was as if his ears were working again, all of a sudden. The sound made him feel better. In spite of this terrible thing that had happened, still the birds could sing.

"Look, James. Look!" William let out a scream of delight. He was pointing to the top of the hill.

James looked – and there was a man, a man he didn't recognise at first. It was a soldier, running out of the morning mist, running down the embankment towards them.

"It's my daddy!" Belle screamed. She pulled away from James and she ran. William was close behind her.

It was their dad, come to get them.

He swung Belle up into his arms, and then William, and held them both close against him.

"James, my son, I am so proud of you," he said, and he pulled James close and hugged him too.

"Come on," their dad said, after a moment. "Let's get away from here."

Belle wrapped her arms around his neck. "Where are we going, Daddy?"

James looked beyond Belle and their dad to the top of the hill. Someone else was standing there now – and it was their mammy, holding out her arms to them.

Their daddy smiled at her and kissed Belle's face. "All of us are together now, just like I promised," he said. "We're going home."

About This Story

We Will Remember Them

In the early hours of the morning of 22nd May 1915, a troop train left Larbert station in Scotland. It was transporting over 500 soldiers of the 1st Battalion of the 7th Royal Scots Guards to Liverpool where they would board a ship, *The Aquitaine*. The ship would take them to Gallipoli. The soldiers were on their way to fight in the First World War.

On a remote stretch of line at Quintinshill near Gretna Green, the train was travelling at 80 miles an hour when it struck a local train that had been left standing on the same line. The first carriages shot over the local train, and fire broke out as the gas for the lamps in the train exploded. Thirty seconds after the first impact, an express train came from the opposite direction and struck the wreckage. Engines piled on top of each other, carriages were overturned, there was fire everywhere. The inferno burned for 23 hours.

Out of the 500 soldiers who had been on that train, only 65 were at the roll call later that day. Over 225 soldiers died in the crash, and 246 were badly injured. Almost as many soldiers from the 1st Battalion died at Quintinshill as were killed in the First World War itself. Many were never identified because the roll list was destroyed in the fire.

It was Britain's worst ever rail disaster.

Two signal-men, James Tinsley and George Meakin, were found guilty of culpable homicide and imprisoned.

But here is the strangest part of the story. When the bodies were taken from the train, the bodies of three children were found among all the soldiers. These three children were never identified. No children were reported missing and their bodies were never claimed. No one has ever discovered who these children were. No one knows how they ended up on a troop train. It may be that they stowed away on the train the night before, when it was in a siding in Maryhill in Glasgow.

The children were thought to have come from the Maryhill area and were later buried at the Western Necropolis cemetery in Glasgow. For a long time those children lay in an unmarked grave. In 2011, Billy Buchanan, a councillor and amateur historian from Falkirk, arranged for a memorial to be placed there.

The memorial reads:

THE
LOST CHILDREN
OF MARYHILL

TRAGIC VICTIMS OF

QUINTINSHILL RAIL DISASTER

WHO DIED 22ND MAY 1915

THEY WERE SADLY NEVER NAMED

OR CLAIMED

There are four bodies buried there. The age of the fourth body is unknown. Some people believe there might have been four children.

Don't you think that is a baffling mystery? And such a sad one, too. Who could those children have been? Why did no one claim them? How did they get on that train, and why were they there?

Stars Shall Be Bright is my idea of who the three children were and what might have happened to them.

Perhaps you might have an idea of your own. Perhaps you could write your own story.

For the Fallen

With proud thanksgiving, a mother for her children,
England mourns for her dead across the sea.
Flesh of her flesh they were, spirit of her spirit,
Fallen in the cause of the free.

Solemn the drums thrill; Death august and royal
Sings sorrow up into immortal spheres,
There is music in the midst of desolation
And a glory that shines upon our tears.

They went with songs to the battle, they were young,
Straight of limb, true of eye, steady and aglow.
They were staunch to the end against odds uncounted;
They fell with their faces to the foe.

They shall grow not old, as we that are left grow old:
Age shall not weary them, nor the years condemn.
At the going down of the sun and in the morning
We will remember them.

They mingle not with their laughing comrades again;

They sit no more at familiar tables of home;

They have no lot in our labour of the day-time;

They sleep beyond England's foam.

But where our desires are and our hopes profound,

Felt as a well-spring that is hidden from sight,

To the innermost heart of their own land they are known

As the stars are known to the Night;

As the stars that shall be bright when we are dust,

Moving in marches upon the heavenly plain;

As the stars that are starry in the time of our darkness,

To the end, to the end, they remain.

This poem by Robert Laurence Binyon was published in The Times *on 21st September 1914.*

Our books are tested
for children and young people by
children and young people.

Thanks to everyone who consulted on
a manuscript for their time and effort in
helping us to make our books better
for our readers.